llama llama time to share

Anna Dewdney

SCHOLASTIC INC.

Llama Llama playing trains,
driving trucks, and flying planes.

Someone's at the door . . . who is it?
Brand new neighbors come to visit.

Llama, this is Nelly Gnu.

Look!

She has a dolly, too.

Mrs. Gnu, would you like tea?

Come and have a cup with me.

You two kids can play in there. . . .

And Llama,
don't forget to **share.**

Trains and trucks and puzzles, too.
What's the Gnu girl want to do?
Play with kitchen? Build with blocks?
Llama opens up his box.

Nelly starts to build a town.
Llama Llama starts to frown. . . .

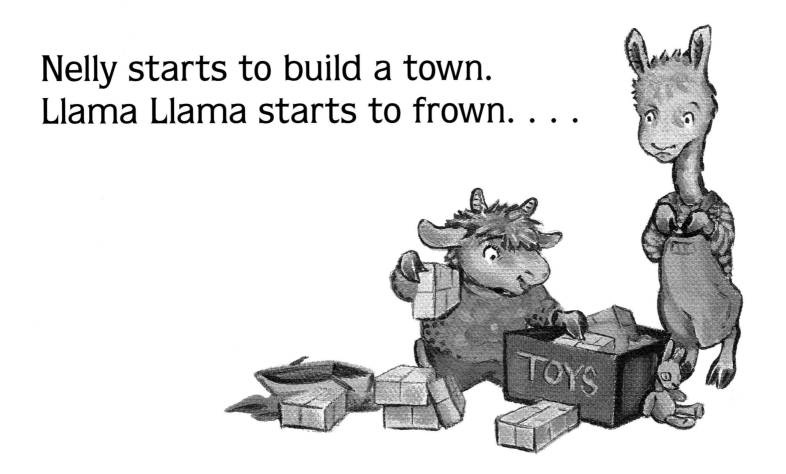

Nelly Gnu makes walls and stairs.
Llama watches from a chair.

Nelly stacks the blocks up high.
Fuzzy Llama wants to try.

It's a castle! Make it tall.
Fuzzy Llama jumps the wall!

Build a tower. Make a moat.
Nelly's dolly rows a boat.

What can Llama Llama add?
Maybe sharing's **not** so bad.

Little baby Gnu makes noise.
Mrs. Gnu gets jingly toys.
Baby screams and kicks his feet.
Mama thinks it's time to eat.

Moms are talking,
baby's chewing. . . .

Where's that Gnu girl?
What's **she** doing?

Oh, **disaster!** Dolly drama!

Nelly Gnu has
Fuzzy Llama!

He's not hers! This isn't fair!

Llama DOESN'T

Fuzzy Llama ripped in two . . .
all because of Nelly Gnu!

It's a **llama-mergency!**

Mama! Fix his arm for me!

A bit of thread and good as new . . .
but this is what we're going to do:

I'll put Fuzzy on the stairs
until you're **sure** that you can share.

Nelly's sorry.
Llama, too.

It's time for
something
else to do.

Maybe tractors?

Maybe not.

Like to dress up?

Not a lot.